FOR FRIDA S.T.
FOR BADGER K.H.

Text copyright © 2016 by Sean Taylor
Illustrations copyright © 2016 by Kate Hindley

All rights reserved. No part of this book may be reproduced, transmitted, or stored in an information retrieval system in any form or by any means, graphic, electronic, or mechanical, including photocopying, taping, and recording, without prior written permission from the publisher.

First U.S. edition 2016

Library of Congress Catalog Card Number pending
ISBN 978-0-7636-8119-7

16 17 18 19 20 21 APS 10 9 8 7 6 5 4 3 2 1

Printed in Humen, Dongguan, China

This book was typeset in ThrohandInk.
The illustrations were done in pencil and paint and colored digitally.

Candlewick Press, 99 Dover Street, Somerville, Massachusetts 02144

visit us at www.candlewick.com

CANDLEWICK PRESS

Don't Call Me CHOOCHIE POOH!

ILLUSTRATED BY

SEAN TAYLOR   KATE HINDLEY

TINY TINKER

PUPPY CONDITIONER

Eau de Pup

I might be little,
but I'm not one of those
silly dogs you see.

Because I'm little, my owner gives me heart-shaped Mini Puppy Treats.

They're the *most* embarrassing things you've ever seen.

CHOOCHIE

And last week we were walking down the street and she said to me,

Come on, Ickle Pickle WOOF WOOF!

Did you know that other dogs can laugh
and make you feel very small? Well, they can.

Outside the supermarket,
she said,

Wait here,
my INCY wincy
CUPCAKE!

Then, when she came out,
she picked me up and she *kissed* me
so everyone could see. And she said,
"Off we go, CHOOCHIE POOH!"

Be honest. Do I look like
I should be called *that*?

I gave her an angry look
as if to tell her,

DON'T call me CHOOCHIE POOH!

But I don't think I'm
good at angry looks
because she said,

You're hungry, aren't you?
LOOK, I've bought you
some Mini Puppy Treats.

Then she put me
in her handbag!

What can you do?

We stopped at the park on the way home.
There were other dogs there.

AND CHIEF, WHO'S VERY BIG AND USED TO BE A <u>POLICE</u> <u>DOG</u>!

They were running around, barking, getting muddy, and doing normal dog things.

Meanwhile I felt like a Mini-Puppy-Treat-eating-Choochie-Pooh in a handbag! I thought they'd never ever want to play with me.

But I was wrong!
Because Chief looked at me
as if to say, *"Come on!"*

So I did. And it was . . .

AWESOME!

We played It's My Stick!
(The main rule is you have to growl
as if you're really angry,
even though you're not.)

Then we played Dogs and Sausages!
(This has complicated rules
that would take a long time to explain.)

And Puddle Jumping!
(This game doesn't have any rules at all.)

I felt more excited than you can even imagine.
It was like being a regular dog!

What's more, Rusty, Bandit, and Chief
all looked at me as if to say, "Come back
and play any time you want!"

Then,

disaster struck . . .

My owner called out,

I wanted to jump into a pit full of crocodiles.

I waited for my new friends to laugh and make me feel very small. But then . . . Rusty's owner said,

Time to go home, **JIGGINS WIGGINS CUDDLE Pie!**

And Bandit's owner said,

come on, **YOU LITTLE CUTIE PATOOTIE!**

Then Chief's owner said,

Let's go, HUNKY PUNKY PUMPKIN BOTTOM!

I looked at my friends.

They looked at me.

We all looked at each other,
as if to say,

"What can you do?"

I play with them all the time now.

And I have to say that after all
the running and barking and
big dogs' games . . .

even Mini Puppy Treats
taste quite good.